PHONICS CHAPTER BOOK 5

Let's Go on a Museum Hunt

by Francie Alexander and Nancy Hechinger
Illustrated by Anthony Lewis

Scholastic Inc.
New York   Toronto   London   Auckland   Sydney

Copyright © 1998 by Scholastic Inc.
Scholastic *Phonics Chapter Books* is a trademark of Scholastic Inc.
All rights reserved. Published by Scholastic Inc.
Printed in the U.S.A.
ISBN 0-590-76457-8
5 6 7 8 9 10   14   04 03 02 01 00 99 98

Dear Teacher/Family Member,

Research has shown that phonics is an essential strategy for figuring out unknown words. Early readers need the opportunity to learn letter sounds and how to blend or put them together to make words. These skills must be practiced over and over again by reading stories containing words with the sounds being taught.

That's why I'm happy to be an author and Program Coordinator of the **Phonics Chapter Books.** These books provide early readers with playful, fanciful stories in easy-to-manage chapters. More importantly, the words in the stories are controlled for phonics sounds and common sight words. Once sounds and sight words have been introduced, they are continually reviewed and applied in succeeding stories, so children will be able to decode these books—and read them on their own. There is nothing more powerful and encouraging than success.

John Shefelbine
Associate Professor, Reading Education
California State University, Sacramento

CONTENTS

1 Charlie and Kate on the Trail

"Rain, rain, please stay! We are going inside the museum today!" said Charlie and Kate.

This was the day they went to visit Dr. Green. Kate's father drove them. It rained all the way.

When the boy and the girl got to the museum, a man said, "Come in out of the rain. Dr. Green is waiting for you. Go that way."

"Hello!" said Charlie and Kate.
They waited and waited. No one said
hello back.

"Maybe Dr. Green had to go away,"
said Kate. "Let's go."

"Wait, wait!" said Charlie. "I want to
stay. I see a big box with a note."

This is what the note had to say.

Charlie and Kate,
I had to go,
But I need your help today.
See the things in the box?
They must be put away!
Please stay.

Dr. Green

They raised the lid on the box.

"This looks like fun! Let's play the game," said Kate. "Let's get on the trail."

"I can't wait!" said Charlie. "Let's go this way."

2 This Hall Is for the Birds

This is what they saw in the box.

They saw an egg.

They saw a bug.

They saw a snakeskin.

They saw a jawbone.

They saw a claw.

They saw a straw.

They saw a key.

"Dr. Green did not tell us where these all go," said Kate.

"Hmm," said Charlie.

"Is that all you can say?" asked Kate.

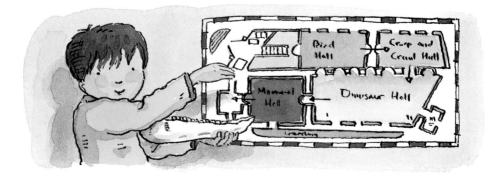

"Look! These things can tell us where they go," said Charlie.

"Hello-o-o, Charlie. You think that jawbone can speak?" Kate said.

"This jawbone calls me to Dinosaur Hall," said Charlie.

"Now I get it. This claw goes on a paw. It may have to go to Mammal Hall," said Kate.

"The egg is for a small bird," said Charlie. "Let's check it out in Bird Hall. Before we go, let's look at the map on the wall."

"Look at all the birds. Some are small. This one is tall," Kate said.

"That nest is too big, but this small nest seems good. Look! There is a red ball and a note in the nest!" said Charlie.

Take out the ball.
Don't let the egg fall.
Lay the egg in the nest.
This place is best.

Dr. Green

Charlie put the egg away.

Then Kate picked up the note. This is what it said on the back.

Around the wall,
In the next hall,
You will see things
That creep and crawl.

"I do not like things that creep and crawl," complained Charlie.

"It will be fine. I like bugs," said Kate.

TO CREEP AND
CRAWL HALL

3 What They Looked at in Creep and Crawl Hall

Charlie and Kate pushed and pulled the box to the next hall.

"This hall gives me the creeps," said Charlie.

They looked in the box to see what to put there. "It must be the bug and the snakeskin," guessed Kate.

Charlie jumped back. "I do not like bugs and snakes," he said. Then he raced off.

Kate smiled and pulled out the snakeskin. "Stay and read this," she called to Charlie.

Sometimes snakes shed their skin. They slide out of it and leave it in the grass.

Kate skipped to a snake case and placed the snakeskin in it. The snakes were not alive.

"Let's see. If we go around this wall, we will get to the bugs," said Kate.

SNAKES

INSECTS

"No way," said Charlie.

"It is fine. They are not alive, just like the one Dr. Green left for us," Kate said. "Look at this display."

Charlie peeked. "Not too bad," he admitted.

"This bug is tan and spotted," noted Kate. "I think it is a beetle." Kate investigated and saw a place for it in the display. She put it inside the case. Charlie helped.

"I am glad that we are done here. I want to see Dinosaur Hall. That will be the best of all," Charlie insisted.

Then he saw a note from Dr. Green.

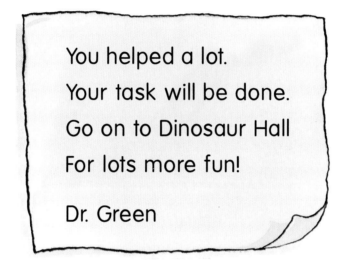

You helped a lot.
Your task will be done.
Go on to Dinosaur Hall
For lots more fun!

Dr. Green

4 They Go to Dinosaur Hall

"Follow me. I am feeling brave," said Charlie. "I will show you the way."

"Slow down," said Kate. "I have the box this time. I want to look at some stuff on the way."

"Oh, this is so neat!" exclaimed Charlie when they got there. "I know what to put here." He held the jawbone up and showed it to Kate.

"It is big and a little bit yellow. Where can it go?" asked Kate.

"I don't know, but I like Dinosaur Hall the best," said Charlie.

TO DINOSAUR HALL

Kate and Charlie looked around.
They saw a girl and her mother looking,
too. The girl had a bow.

When the girl bent to look in a
display case, her bow fell. Kate went
to pick it up for her. It was then that
Kate saw a note beside the bow.
The note had a fold, and on the
outside it said "OPEN ME."

The girl and Charlie both looked on
while Kate opened the note.

You are as good as gold.
Put the jawbone in the case,
Then go to the next place.

Dr. Green

"Oh, no," said Charlie. "I like it here in Dinosaur Hall. When I grow up, I will have my own desk at the museum and a job like Dr. Green's."

"Let's go," said Kate. "I will show you the way to Mammal Hall. That is a good place for a claw."

5 A Claw, a Straw, and a Key

The kids went quickly to Mammal Hall. "The claw will go here," said Kate.

"What exactly is a mammal?" asked Charlie.

"We study mammals in school," said Kate. "The mother mammal feeds milk to her baby."

Just as Kate said this, she saw a display on baby mammals.

"Oh! The baby fox is very fluffy and pretty," said Kate.

"The baby monkey looks really funny," said Charlie. "Look! The baby seal is so cute. Can a sea animal be a mammal?"

"Yes. I had to study that, too," said Kate. "Can we go? We still need a place for a claw."

"There must be twenty mammals here. The claw is too small for that big angry cat," said Charlie.

"The claw is too big for the chipmunk," Kate said.

"The claw is for the dog!" they both said at once.

They were happy to set the claw
in its place. Then they saw a note.

> Charlie really likes the dinosaurs.
> Kate really likes the bugs.
> In the next hall is someone
> Who likes to sing and read and hug.
>
> Dr. Green

"What do we do with the straw and
the key?" asked Charlie.

"We will see," said Kate.

6 The Goal

Kate and Charlie saw many neat things in the Hall of Humans. They looked at how humans lived a long time ago and how they live today.

"We still do not know where to put the straw and the key," Charlie groaned.

"How will we meet our goal and help Dr. Green?" asked Kate.

"Look there! I see a lock," said Charlie. "Hand me the key."

The key fit. The lock opened. They went outside.

It had stopped raining. The sun was out, and there was a rainbow. Dr. Green was next to an oak tree. She had a picnic basket.

"You did it! You met the goal!" said Dr. Green. "Now get your coats and come out."

"You helped with the notes," said the kids.

"You did the real job. I was just the coach," said Dr. Green. "It was a way to show you what I do."

Dr. Green explained, "I am a scientist. Scientists look at things in the world, like you looked at the things in the museum here today. It is fun, like your hunt, and it is my job."

"I want to be a scientist at the museum and have my own desk," said Charlie. "That is my goal!"

"I want to be a scientist and roam the world looking for things for museums," said Kate.

"You are on the road to reaching
your goals," said Dr. Green. "And I can
still be your coach. I will loan you things
to read, and you can come back here
many more times."

They sat next to the oak tree and
had their picnic.

"I see what to do with this straw now," said Charlie.

"This is yummy," said Kate.

Dr. Green then told them a story about a very, very old map she once saw on a boat trip to Mexico...

PHONICS

Decodable Words With the Phonic Elements

1 **ai** raised
trail
wait

ay away
day
play
say
stay
way

-ain rain

2 **-all** all
ball
calls
fall
hall
small
tall
wall

-aw crawl
jawbone
claw
paw
saw
straw

3 **-ed/d/** called
smiled

/ed/ admitted
insisted
noted
spotted

/t/ helped
jumped
peeked
placed
pushed
raced
skipped

4 **o** oh
open
both
fold
gold
go
so

ow own
bow
follow
grow
show
slow
yellow

5 **y** baby
fluffy
funny
happy
pretty
really
study
twenty
very

ey key
monkey

-ly exactly
quickly

6 **oa** oak
boat
coach
coats
goal
groaned
loan
road
roam